Mary has spent most of her life living in Swansea, in Wales. Several years were spent living in Hamburg, in Germany, with her late husband, Heinz, and daughter, Anna, where her fascination with doll making began. Mary plays the organ, speaks fluent German, loves travelling abroad and is a prolific reader.

I dedicate this book to the memory of
Captain Heinz Bessenich
1941-2004


without whom I would never have become acquainted with the beautiful country of Germany, spoken the language fluently and amassed a wealth of extraordinary memories.


You enabled me to write this book.

Thank you for everything

Mary Bessenich

# THE ADVENTURES OF ROSE

AUSTIN MACAULEY PUBLISHERS™

LONDON • CAMBRIDGE • NEW YORK • SHARJAH

A CIP catalogue record for this title is available from the British Library.

ISBN 9781398452206 (Paperback)
ISBN 9781398452213 (ePub e-book)

www.austinmacauley.com

First Published 2022
Austin Macauley Publishers Ltd®
1 Canada Square
Canary Wharf
London
E14 5AA

It was a wonderful morning in the beautiful old town of Rothenburg in Bavaria. Rothenburg was considered to be the quaintest place in all of Germany with its fairy-tale atmosphere of narrow cobbled streets, half-timbered houses, charming little shops and streets full of exquisite hanging baskets, offering a kaleidoscope of colour in all of its streets. The sun was shining, the birds were singing and there wasn't a cloud in the sky. Hans threw back his bed covers, put on his clothes, and went downstairs into his workshop. Whilst he was waiting for the coffee to brew, Hans opened the windows of his double-fronted timber house and waved across the street to the violin maker Jacob, who was already hard at work in his workshop.

Jacob was twenty-six years old, two years older than Hans, and he also loved sitting by the open windows making his beautiful violins. Both Hans and Jacob were highly skilled craftsmen in their own right and both strived to attain perfection in all they created. When Jacob became a father to little Klara, Hans made a beautiful ceramic doll to celebrate her birth. He spent days and weeks creating the perfect doll for Jacob's daughter and then when it was finally finished, he painted the name *Klara,* on the nape of its neck and underneath, the date she was born. Jacob was delighted at this unexpected show of friendship towards him and from that moment on both men enjoyed a gentle friendship, always shouting out "Guten Morgen" to each other every morning from their open windows.

The village was kept scrupulously clean by its inhabitants, as the villagers were proud German folk. Hans had been brought up in this charming little village and all the local shopkeepers knew and loved him. The fact that he had continued to run the doll making business was a source of great pride to his grandfather and also to his father. Arthritis had forced his father to retire early from the craft he had so loved. This gesture in itself had endeared him even more to the villagers as they knew that other opportunities could have been seized by Hans. He was a bright young lad and had contemplated going to the University in Heidelberg to

7

study medicine, but Hans had felt a pang of nostalgia when he thought of the workshop closing and everything his grandfather had built up gone forever.

Hans still bought his daily brötchen from Frau Schäfer on the corner of the same street where his workshop was, as did his parents and his grandparents before him. Frau Schäfer was eighty-three but still got up at 4am to ensure that the villagers had plenty of vollkornbrot, brötchen, pretzels and küchen to wake up to. Her bakery smelt delicious!

This morning Hans was going to start work on a porcelain doll. He had already decided on her name. She was to be named Rose.

# The Creation of Rose

Hans washed his hands thoroughly. He placed a blue heavy-duty plastic cloth on his table and assembled everything to make his porcelain dough. He mixed kaolin, quartz, feldspar and water together, and then poured the liquid mixture into a plaster mould that he had made the previous day. Hans left the porcelain in the mould to dry, waiting for it to develop a leathery appearance. Once it was ready, he placed it in the firing oven.

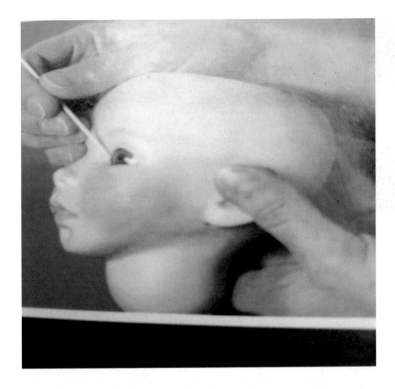

Just before he completed stitching up the doll, he carved a little heart out of some porcelain dough he had leftover. When it had set, he picked it up and was about to place it inside the doll but then thought better of it. He didn't want Rose to have a heart of stone – he wanted her to have a soft heart. He searched around the workshop for some scrap of material he could use and found a lovely piece of soft red velvet. He cut it into the shape of a tiny heart and stitched it carefully inside her. This doll would be able to feel joy, pain, heartache, and love. He had never done this before with any other doll but he felt compelled to do it with Rose.

When he had finished, he sat her on a piece of wood and placed her on a shelf. He pulled up a chair and sat opposite her and gazed with wonder at what he had achieved. She was a beautiful doll. He'd done a great job. His grandfather would have been proud of him as would his father be when he next visited the workshop. His final task would be to ask his grandmother to make Rose some beautiful clothes. His grandmother had been a professional seamstress in her younger days and still enjoyed making dolls clothes for Hans although now her hands were severely arthritic.

Sure enough, a week later his grandmother walked slowly down to his workshop using her walking stick, tapped on the door and handed Hans a brown paper package. She waved across to Jacob who was tuning a violin and then she walked into Hans's workshop. Hans opened the parcel and held up the beautifully made clothes. "Oma, du bist ein Engel" (You're an angel). His grandmother hugged him and they both sat down and had coffee with some pretzels from Frau Schäfer's bakery. Mmm, they were delicious.

Once Hans had made about four dolls, he would contact his list of retailers and ask them whether they were looking to replenish their stock. His best customer was Frau Winklemann, who had a beautiful shop in the *Altstadt* in Munich. Her shop attracted a lot of tourists, whose children loved both the boy dolls and the girl dolls dressed in the traditional Bavarian costume. Frau Winklemann's shop was like an Aladdin's cave. There were dolls of every shape and size, large and small cuckoo clocks, embroidered tea towels, wooden puppets, pretty tablecloths, music boxes, Dolls Houses, Steiff teddy bears, lederhosen for young boys, exquisitely embroidered blouses for young girls, ornate tea services, cake stands and lots and lots of other quaint curiosities. It was a children's paradise!

Hans was very fond of Frau Winklemann. She was a friendly, warm hearted lady who always made a huge fuss of him when he arrived at her shop with his delivery. She opened the boxes very carefully and when she looked at these exquisite little beings for the first time her eyes filled with tears. She held each doll in her hands with such reverence and affection that Hans used to feel immense satisfaction in these moments. Frau Winklemann always offered him coffee after the delivery had been opened and checked and Hans would sit at the back of the shop, sipping the hot coffee, watching customers come in wide-eyed and fascinated as they entered this magic kingdom.

Hans watched as Frau Winklemann carefully placed Rose on display in the shop window. The other three dolls she placed on shelves in the shop. The window was well lit and Rose took pride of place next to an enormous Dolls House that had been made by a carpenter of great repute in Heidelberg. The doll's house was by far the focal point of the window display as the front of it had been opened to show the beautiful furnishings of each room. Miniature chandeliers were hanging from the ceilings, together with tiny books, a grand piano, an English doll's pram, four-poster beds, a children's nursery with cots, tiny toys, baby clothes and many other beautifully handcrafted objects. It was truly magnificent. The cabinetmaker (*Kunsttischler*) Johannes Fischer was also a good friend of Frau Winklemann's and he had told her that his dolls house had been based upon the model that had been made for Queen Mary by Edwin Lutyens back in 1921. Johannes had stood in absolute awe and wonder when he'd seen it for the first time at Windsor Castle some years ago. He remained there for two hours, studying each individual piece in detail and afterwards, as he walked out of the castle, he knew that it had been one of the best days of his life.

Frau Winklemann prided herself on her window displays. Many local people who were out shopping would take their children to admire the exquisitely decorated window. The children's faces were a sight to behold as their eyes fixed firstly on the magnificent dolls house and then on everything else arrayed around it. The doll's house was always a strong talking point amongst the folk in the *Altstadt.* Frau Winklemann always ensured that the window was brightly lit during the night and people couldn't help but stop for a while gazing at the beauty in front of them, before walking on to find somewhere nice to eat.

Hans had finished his coffee and was just about to get up from his seat when a very well-dressed man entered the shop holding the hand of his little daughter. Hans thought fleetingly that the man looked similar to Daniel Craig. The man walked purposefully towards the small counter situated in the far corner of the shop and asked to see the doll in the window. Hans couldn't believe his ears! Frau Winklemann had only just put Rose in the window! Good Heavens!

Frau Winklemann went to the front window and picking up Rose very carefully brought her over to where the father and daughter were standing. She placed her gently on the counter. The little girl gasped. Her father smiled and asked Frau Winklemann whether the doll had a name. She said that the doll maker had painted the name *Rose* on the nape of its neck.

Hans listened to the conversation intently and secretly hoped that the man wouldn't buy Rose. Hans had grown to love this little doll, having spent many weeks painting beautiful features onto her face to make her look exceptionally lovely. Each day he had thought of yet another idea to enhance her even more. The father asked his daughter if she was sure that this was the present she wanted for her ninth birthday and the little girl nodded her head. She gazed up at her father and squeezed his hand.

Hans suddenly felt his stomach churn. He couldn't understand why he felt like this. Rose was just another doll, one of many he had made over the years. He watched as Frau Winkelmann wrapped his beloved Rose in pale pink tissue paper, and then placed her in brown paper, taping the ends of the parcel firmly in place. Frau Winkelmann placed the package in a pretty carrier bag and handed it to the little girl.

"Wie heisst Du mein Schatz?" asked Frau Winklemann, addressing the beautifully dressed little girl. "Charlotte," the little girl replied. Frau Winklemann smiled. The little girl didn't look unlike the doll her father had just bought her. It was an extraordinary likeness.

Charlotte and her father left the shop with Rose. Hans stood at the back of the shop and felt slightly sick. He had the strangest premonition that Rose was going to have a tough time. He looked deep in thought as he handed Frau Winkelmann his empty coffee mug. He thanked her for the coffee and left the shop. Frau Winkelmann watched Hans walk slowly back to his van, observing his pained expression. She knew what had happened. She had seen it with several other doll makers. They simply became too close to their own creations, as they often mirrored their own anxieties in the faces of these little people. She thought she would have felt thrilled at having sold the doll so quickly but she spent the rest of the day feeling sad. She kept seeing the sadness in the face of Hans. She would be glad to go home tonight.

As Hans walked back to his little van, which he had parked around the corner from the shop, he suddenly smiled to himself. He remembered that he had painted the name "Rose" on the nape of her neck but also his name and address on the sole of Rose's right foot. Maybe they would be reunited one day, and clutching onto that thought he got into his little van and began his journey home.

# Charlotte
# Rose's first owner

Charlotte lived with her parents in a large house just outside Hamburg in a village called Blankenese. They had recently returned from a short trip to Munich where her mother had wanted to visit the Christmas markets. Once home, they unpacked their suitcases, ate a light meal and got ready for bed. Charlotte took the parcel out of the carrier bag, carefully removing the brown paper and then gently picking up Rose out of the pink tissue paper.

Charlotte's bedroom was like a fairy-tale. The wallpaper was covered in pink cherubs with trees, forests, birds and flowers. The ceiling was painted pale pink with a beautiful glass chandelier hanging from it adorned with mint green rosebuds. Her bed was a four-poster, draped in pink velvet, with lots of teddy bears and dolls arrayed neatly on it. Her curtains were elegant, made from the same pink velvet material as the bed drapes, tied back with ornate cream tassels. The carpet was a very pale cream. Charlotte looked around her bedroom for a suitable place for her new doll and decided to place her on her pink velvet bedroom chair. Rose looked absolutely gorgeous. Charlotte got into bed and looked across at Rose. "Gute Nacht meine liebe Rose. Schlaf gut." Charlotte switched off her lamp and hugged the bedclothes tightly around her. She couldn't wait to show Rose to her best friend Sophia tomorrow.

It was Saturday and Sophia was getting dropped off by her mother to spend the day with Charlotte. Charlotte ran down the stairs to welcome her, giving her a big hug. Sophia's mother had made them her delicious *Apfelstrudel* and brought a carton of thick cream for them to pour over it. Sophia handed the basket to Charlotte's mother. They all waved to Sophia's mother from the front door, blowing her kisses and shouting "Vielen Dank" as she drove off, and then they closed the door. Charlotte's mother took the basket of *Apfelstrudel* and cream into the kitchen whilst the two girls ran up the stairs laughing and giggling!

Charlotte and Sophia had been friends ever since their first day of primary school. They looked completely different from one another. Charlotte had beautiful chestnut brown hair which she wore in two plaits. She had large brown eyes, very long eyelashes, a pale complexion and cherry red lips but always wore a rather serious expression. Sophia on the other hand had short curly blonde hair, big blue eyes, lots of freckles and was always laughing! They were devoted to one another. Neither child had been fortunate to have any siblings so they felt like sisters. It was a beautiful friendship.

Sophia fell in love with Rose the minute she set eyes on her. She had never seen such a beautiful doll. She studied her little face intently and wondered why the doll maker had given her such a sad expression. Sophia thought the doll looked worried and anxious but Charlotte didn't share Sophia's opinion. She said that Rose's face was not sad but thoughtful.

Charlotte and Sophia sat down later to a big plate of warm *Apfelstrudel* with a huge topping of thick cream. It was delicious. Charlotte told Sophia about their short trip to Munich and the Christmas markets. She described the shop where they had bought Rose. "Oh Sophia, you wouldn't have believed it. There was a huge dolls house in the window and it had the most amazing things in it." Sophia listened in awe as Charlotte described all the rooms in the doll's house and the beautifully crafted pieces of tiny furniture, the pram, the grand piano, the chandeliers, baby clothes, books, etc.

She said that Rose was sitting just to the right of the doll's house and she knew, as soon as she saw her, that she had to have her. She told Sophia that her father had asked her if she was absolutely sure that this was what she wanted for her ninth birthday and she had told her father that it was. She told Sophia that the lady in the shop was really nice and had wrapped the doll up ever so carefully and then had asked her what her name was.

After listening to Charlotte, Sophia thought she might suggest to her parents that they visit this wonderful shop and maybe find a doll as lovely as Rose for herself. Her birthday was a long way off though, but she could wait. A doll as lovely as Rose was worth waiting for.

Rose spent the next ten years with Charlotte. The first few years were lovely as Charlotte played with her most days or took her to bed and cuddled her before she fell asleep. As Charlotte became older Rose spent most of her time sitting on one of the bedroom windowsills. It was a lonely existence for her as Charlotte had lost interest in her and just glanced across at her from time to time whilst listening to music, studying or chatting with Sophia.

On her 19th birthday, Charlotte left home to begin her studies at the University of Heidelberg. She was going to study medicine. Sophia had also decided to do the same so the two friends left to embark on a wonderful journey together, which would ultimately culminate in them becoming doctors. Both their parents were very proud.

As Charlotte loaded her suitcases into the boot of her father's car, her mother asked her about all her old toys which were now in a big cardboard box in the attic. Charlotte said they could all be given to the charity shop. Her mother smiled. That's exactly what she was hoping to hear!

Rose had been sitting in the cardboard box for the last 4 years. It was cold and dark in the attic and she hated it. She had felt so many different emotions sitting in the attic: sadness, helplessness, betrayed but most of all lonely.

One morning, she heard the attic door being opened and Charlotte's father was standing at the top of a ladder peering into the darkness. He switched on his torch, took hold of the cardboard box with both hands and carried it carefully down the ladder. She felt a blast of cold air and realised she was outdoors. The box she was in was placed on the back seat of a car before they headed away from the house.

# The Charity Shop

Rose was placed on a shelf in the middle of the shop. The shop was full of old shoes, old clothes, old toys, broken tables and all sorts of bric-a-brac. It was quite clear to Rose that this was a shop where people brought things that they didn't want anymore. How could they have done this to her? She thought back to how lovingly Hans had made her in his workshop all those years ago. That had been a very special time for her because she had felt loved. The workshop had always been a happy place with the windows wide open in summer and passers-by popping their heads through the window to say "Guten Morgen" to Hans. This shop smelt stuffy and looked shabby and there were huge cobwebs in all the corners. She watched as people came into the shop, treading on clothes that had fallen onto the floor. She felt terrified and degraded. Why on earth had they brought her here?

Then her worst nightmare happened. A little boy came into the shop with his mother, looked at Rose, picked her up and threw her onto the floor. His mother didn't notice what he had done and continued looking through the clothes on hangers. More and more people started coming into the shop and kept stepping on Rose or they just kicked her to the side as they browsed through all the bric-a-brac. She felt a sharp pain in her tummy.

Finally, it was time for the shop to close and all the people disappeared. The two ladies who ran the shop started picking up all the clothes which had fallen onto the floor and then one of them noticed Rose. The lady picked her up, and realising how filthy she was, decided that they would never be able to sell her in such a poor state. She put her in a black bag along with other items that were too badly damaged to sell. She placed the bag outside the shop to be picked up by the rubbish collectors the following morning.

Rose felt terrified.

# The Rubbish Collector

In the early hours of the following morning, Rose felt the bag being lifted up. She had lain against a plastic tractor and some smelly clothes all night. She couldn't breathe. The noise from the huge refuse truck was frightening and she could hear lots of men's voices. Suddenly the black bag split open and Rose tumbled out onto the pavement. One of the men ran back and picked her up, ready to throw her onto the truck but his colleague shouted to him to put the doll somewhere safe. He told him he would give it to his daughter. The other refuse collector looked puzzled as the doll looked so shabby. He threw her onto the front seat of the truck. Rose had been saved.

After Helmut had driven the refuse truck back to the depot he removed his overalls, put on his normal clothes and made his way home on the bus. Helmut and his family lived in Altona, a few miles from where Charlotte lived. Altona was full of high-rise apartment blocks and was not a very nice area. They were happy enough living on the ninth floor and his wife Elizabeth kept their small flat clean and tidy. His daughter Marie was seven years old and was so very sweet and loving. What Helmut and his wife didn't know was that Marie often got bullied in primary school because she was very softly spoken and well mannered. Helmut and Elizabeth were both quiet hardworking people and Elizabeth cleaned houses for wealthy people in Hamburg, mainly those living on the Elbchaussee and in Blankenese.

When Helmut arrived home, he told Elizabeth about the doll. He had placed it outside on their little balcony, as she was filthy. Elizabeth couldn't understand why Helmut had brought this doll home, as she was sure Marie wouldn't like her. However, when Marie returned from school her father told her that he had retrieved a little doll from the pavement that day and that she was on the balcony. Marie walked onto the balcony. When she looked at Rose her face dropped. What on earth had happened to this doll she wondered? Marie took Rose into her bedroom which was very shabby. All the furniture was brown and the carpet was threadbare but it was clean. Marie gently removed all Rose's clothes plus her socks and shoes. She filled a bowl with hot soapy water and taking a clean flannel she carefully washed Rose's face, her hands, her arms, her feet and her legs. Her little body had a crack across her tummy where someone must have stepped on her. Marie continued to gently wash the grime off Rose until she was beautifully clean. She kept talking to her very softly as she gently wiped the flannel over her eyelids and ears. Next she started on the clothes. She filled another bowl with hot water and some washing powder and immersed all the dirty clothes into the soapy water. She rubbed the dress hard with her little hands until the water turned grey. She then used some soap to get it really clean and then poured the dirty water down the sink. She filled another bowl with fresh cold water and rinsed the clothes thoroughly. Rose's hair had miraculously stayed in place over the years. Her two plaits were intact and her hair looked beautiful after Marie had brushed off all the dust. Marie wrapped Rose in a fluffy towel and put her in her bed to get warm. The clothes would be dry by the morning and Marie would ask her mother to iron them. Tomorrow this doll would look lovely again.

Marie wished that this could happen to her when she was bullied so that she could come home from school and the sadness she felt could simply be washed away. If only life were that simple, she thought. Wouldn't it be lovely, if grief and sadness could disappear by having a hot bath? You just removed the plug and all the bad stuff disappeared down the plughole and left you feeling completely renewed.

The following morning was Saturday. Elizabeth had only one call to do on the Elbchaussee. It was a very elegant top floor apartment owned by a sea captain who lived there with his wife Mary and their little daughter Anna. He was a kind man although sometimes he could be a little gruff but he always gave her a lot more than her hourly rate of pay. If he had just returned from one of his trips he would always bring back a little gift for Marie. Elizabeth liked him very much.

She would never forget being in the toy section of a large department store, where the captain was buying a doll's pram for Anna. Elizabeth was hiding behind some large toys. A little boy quite shabbily dressed was standing near the captain, holding a teddy bear in his hand and begging his mother to buy it for him. The mother was explaining to him that she couldn't afford to buy it as it was very expensive and told him to put it back straight away. The little boy was distraught. Elizabeth watched as the captain took the teddy bear from the little boy and paid for the doll's pram and the teddy bear on his card. The mother looked completely amazed as he handed the teddy bear back to her little son. The little boy was thrilled. The captain took hold of the doll's pram and walked out of the shop without a backward glance at the mother. Elizabeth watched it all with tears in her eyes.

When Elizabeth returned home, Marie had got the ironing board out ready for her mother to iron Rose's clothes. Elizabeth smiled as she took off her coat. "You really love your little Rose don't you Marie?" Marie nodded. Elizabeth picked up each piece of beautifully hand-sewn clothing: the dress, the socks, the petticoat, the lace bloomers and ironed them lovingly as though they belonged to a princess. Marie watched her mother intently as she ironed the little sleeves and the lace around the bloomers, and there wasn't a crease in sight. Elizabeth put them in a neat pile and placed them in Marie's little hands. "Danke Mutti," said Marie and ran into her bedroom. She picked up Rose still wrapped in the fluffy towel and began to carefully put her clothes back on. She spoke gently to her again as she put her freshly washed bloomers on, her socks, her shoes, her petticoat and then finally her lovely dress. Rose looked absolutely gorgeous! Marie picked her up and held her close to her. Oh, she smelled delicious! As Marie held Rose closely to her, Rose felt her heart bursting with love for this little girl. Her heart was exploding.

# HANS
# The doll maker

Hans had met a very nice girl from the village nine years after he had watched Rose being sold in Frau Winkelmann's shop in Munich. They had bought themselves a very small house with a cellar just a few doors down from his workshop. They had got married and now had a little boy called Stefan. Stefan was a handsome lad and Hans and his wife Luisa would often dress him up in the traditional Bavarian costume on Sundays and he looked amazing. Hans decided he would make a lifelike doll in the image of Stefan and he would do what he had done all those years ago with Rose. He would give him a little heart.

Unfortunately, his grandmother had died recently so he had asked a very skilled dressmaker in the village if she would make the clothes for the doll. She was delighted to do so as she had been a close friend of his grandmother's and within one week the costume was finished. When Hans and Luisa presented the doll to Stefan he started jumping up and down. He was over the moon! "Ich habe einen Zwillingsbruder!" (I've got a twin brother!) Hans and Luisa laughed. He was absolutely right though. The doll did look like his twin brother. The likeness was truly fantastic.

Seeing how thrilled he was, Hans decided to ask the dressmaker if she would make a matching outfit for a teddy bear. She was delighted to oblige and the outfit was delivered to Hans within a few days. She had produced yet another excellent piece of work. He looked brilliant. Stefan loved it! Stefan decided to call his twin brother Karl.

# Marie

Marie still dreaded going to school even now that she was in grammar school. She was 14 years old. There were two girls in her class who had constantly bullied her throughout primary and junior school and her schoolwork was suffering. They would taunt her in the schoolyard, pull her hair and call her names. It was a living hell. Her parents were a loving couple and she had only known kindness and affection from them and therefore Marie had never felt equipped to deal with such hostility – she simply didn't possess the right tools. She felt sick during every playtime as nobody spoke to her from her class while she stood in a corner pretending to read her book. The bullying and isolation had gone on for so many years but she had never told her parents. The only person she had confided in was her little Rose. She found she could pour out all her worries to Rose when she bathed her. She would place her in the large washbasin and wash her little face and body with a hot soapy flannel. Rose loved these moments. Marie would then put a little nightie on Rose, one that her mother had made from an old sheet, and place her in the wooden crib her father had made. Marie gazed at her with such wonder and love. It was a miracle that she had fallen out of that black bag on the day her father was working that particular shift. It had been fate.

One day a new girl arrived in her class. She was very pretty with short blonde hair and big blue eyes with a face that was sharp and birdlike. Her name was Theresa. Marie and Theresa hit it off immediately and became inseparable. Marie had told Theresa everything about the two bullies and that without her little doll at home she would have gone completely mad. Theresa listened to these stories and felt anger grow inside her. Marie was the sweetest girl she had ever met: loyal, caring, kind and loving. She really didn't deserve this. Frau Schmidt, the class teacher, was secretly thrilled at the friendship between the two girls, as she knew Marie had suffered from constant bullying. She was pleased to see Marie finally smiling.

One morning when the school bell rang, everyone flocked out of the classroom into the play yard. Marie walked out with Theresa and they sat down together under a tree.

After about ten minutes, one of the bullies starting walking across to where they both sat talking. She came very close to Theresa's face and told her not to talk to Marie as her father was a rubbish collector and he stank. Marie felt her eyes brimming with tears and her face became hot. At that moment she thought of her mother, witnessing this scene and how upset she would be. She bit her bottom lip and there was a quiet noise of thunder in her ears. She felt as though she were dying inside. Her father. Her dear lovely father, who had rescued little Rose from being thrown into the refuse truck. She saw his kind face in her mind and her hands became clammy. Theresa looked at the bully who was thin-lipped and fat and felt something snap inside her. She got up from the grass, raised her hand in the air and slapped the girl so hard across the face that her hand was burning. The girl screamed and looked aghast, holding her hand against her cheek and gasping. "How dare you speak to Marie like that? HOW DARE YOU!" yelled Theresa. The bully looked stunned at this unexpected show of fury and defiance and felt humiliated and defeated. All the children in the yard just stopped what they were doing and stared at the three girls.

Marie watched this ugly scene with her mouth wide open. Frau Schmidt came running across the yard looking perplexed and saw immediately the bright red handprint on the bully's face. "Ach, du lieber Himmel. What happened here?"

The bully looked down at the floor and said very quietly, "Nothing Frau Schmidt. Nothing at all." Theresa didn't take her eyes off the girl. Her face was etched in pure hatred for this horrible girl who had caused so much suffering to Marie over the years. The message was crystal clear. The bully walked slowly past Frau Schmidt, her cheek now badly swollen, and retreated into the classroom, followed by the rest of the class. Nobody spoke. Theresa and Marie were the last to walk back into the classroom and they sat at their desks. The atmosphere in the classroom was tense. The lesson slowly resumed and the incident was never referred to again and Frau Schmidt never reported it.

That evening, Marie went home and told Rose everything that had happened. Marie hugged Rose to her, smoothing her little head of hair and playing with her plaits. Rose felt such enormous relief, knowing that her beloved Marie would not suffer in school anymore. She had always hoped that the situation would improve and now it finally had. Theresa had come into Marie's life. Everything would be better now. Rose felt happier than ever.

During the course of the next few years, Marie grew into a confident young lady. She excelled in her schoolwork. The two bullies had left school very early on to obtain mundane jobs in the town and Marie stayed on in school until she was ready for college. The friendship with Theresa continued well into adulthood. They would grow old together. She always felt truly grateful that their paths had crossed all those years ago and that the friendship had been truly cemented on that fateful day in the schoolyard. Theresa had enabled her to enjoy her school years and go on to attain excellent grades. Their friendship would endure until the grave.

# Charlotte

Charlotte completed her studies at the University of Heidelberg. She was now a qualified doctor. Sophia had decided she wanted to work in a hospital somewhere in Germany and Charlotte was going to go to Zambia to work at a mission hospital to help with the treatment of malnourished children. They had both worked very hard over the past five years and now a bright new future was opening up for both of them. On the day Charlotte was flying to Zambia, Sophia came to the airport to say goodbye. They hugged each other tightly and wished one another lots of good luck. Sophia's last words to her friend were "Stay safe." They would never see each other again.

# Jade
## Marie's niece

When Marie was 23 years old she became a primary school teacher. She had always yearned for a brother or a sister but sadly it was not to be. She realised that her strong attachment to Rose was probably due to her lack of siblings and also to the fact that her early years in school had been so unpleasant. When her auntie had given birth to Jade eight years ago, she was thrilled and had doted on the little girl.

Her aunt and uncle were very well-to-do and Jade was lavished with expensive clothes and toys. Despite these trappings of wealth, Jade had always loved Rose. Every time the family visited Marie's parents, Jade would run into Marie's bedroom and bring the doll into the living room and play with her.

When the time came for Marie to move out to be closer to the school where she worked, she told Jade that she could have Rose as a gift. Jade threw her arms around Marie and kissed her warmly. "Danke, Tante Marie," she whispered. She hugged Rose tightly.

A year later, Jade's parents decided to go on holiday. They had always wanted to go to Morocco so they booked a 7 night stay in the city of Marrakech. Jade had insisted on taking Rose with her although her mother was not very happy about it. However, Jade had her way and Rose was packed very carefully in the suitcase.

Upon their arrival in Marrakech, they were taken by taxi to a beautiful Riad near the centre of the city. Owing to the narrow alleyways, the taxi driver dropped them as near as he could and then they had to walk the rest of the way. Jade was fascinated with all the sights and smells. She passed donkeys laden with fruit, pulled along by men wearing long gowns with hoods (a djellaba). She saw shops with enormous baskets of spices and herbs outside on the pavement. She peered through the gates of a little primary school where the children were playing in the schoolyard until her parents called out to her to hurry along. She loved this place!

They continued walking through another labyrinth of alleyways until they finally arrived at the Riad. It had a huge church-like door and there was a man dressed in Moroccan costume sitting on a chair outside. He welcomed them warmly and then opened the enormous door. He led them down a long passageway until they arrived at a smaller door. He brought a key out of his pocket and unlocked the door. He opened it wide and let them all enter first. He followed behind carrying their luggage.

Jade had never seen anything so beautiful in her life. Her parents looked wide-eyed at the extraordinary opulence that greeted them. The lobby was full of huge velvet sofas with embroidered cushions, ornate Turkish rugs, and large Moroccan lanterns dimly lit and at the far end there was a magnificent open courtyard with palm trees, lemon trees and a wonderful fountain in its centre. Dotted around the courtyard were tables and chairs with yellow linen tablecloths, with waiters in Moroccan traditional costume serving guests iced tea. On both sides of the open courtyard were sets of little stone steps leading up to individual suites with their own small balconies overlooking the courtyard. Jade thought she was standing in paradise.

They were handed the bedroom key and their suitcases were carried up to their bedroom via a long twisting stone staircase by a young boy in traditional costume. They climbed up and up and then up again and finally arrived outside their door. The room was large and beautiful containing one double bed and two single beds, Turkish rugs, lanterns, a marble bathroom with thick fluffy towels, hand carved wardrobes and the best of it all was that Rose had a bed for herself!

Later that evening, Jade and her parents plus Rose walked up the final flight of steps and onto the roof terrace. The view over Marrakech was amazing, with the entire city all brightly lit under a starry sky. They went back down the stony staircase and entered the beautiful courtyard to enjoy a tasty lamb tagine whilst listening to a band of local musicians playing. Afterwards, they went upstairs feeling happy and full. Jade tucked Rose into her bed and kissed her goodnight. They all slept well.

The next day, after a hearty breakfast, they strolled through the famous souks, taking care not to get lost in the maze of alleyways. Rose felt very hot and Jade was wiping her little face with a damp flannel that she had brought with her from the room as they walked in the fierce heat. Jade had dressed Rose in a thin

28

cotton blouse and shorts and removed her socks and shoes. Despite the cool clothing Rose still felt hot. They watched skilled craftsmen making leather bags, satchels, purses, wallets and of course their famous pointed slippers. They admired the weavers making beautiful baby cots, tablemats and ornate baskets. They saw the brass and metalworkers producing huge freestanding lanterns and the potters creating the most gorgeous ceramics. It was fascinating. It was like being in another world.

# The Day Rose Disappeared

Jade's parents had booked an excursion to Essaouira, a seaside resort not far from Marrakech. The weather was very hot again and they thought a trip to the seaside would be good. The tour bus was waiting for them on the main road and they got in and greeted everyone on-board and sat down. Rose sat on Jade's lap. Rose always felt very safe when she was with Jade. Jade always held her very tightly to her wherever they went just as Marie had done when she was a little girl. Life had taken the sweetest turn after she had been stuck in Charlotte's attic for years gathering dust. Rose felt blessed.

When they arrived in Essaouira, they headed down to the beach and within minutes they were all splashing in the lovely cool sea. Jade loved it. They had left Rose on the beach wrapped in one of their beach towels. After coming out of the sea Jade's father suggested they do a little boat trip. They hopped onto a motorboat that was just about to leave, bought three tickets from a crewmember, donned their life jackets and then the boat started up. Jade had placed a little sunhat on Rose's head to protect her from the heat and held her tight, wrapping her arms around her. The boat headed off. It was exhilarating to watch the waves and Jade could see them getting further and further from the shore. The beach was now just a little dot behind them as the boat skimmed across the water. After some time the waves suddenly became very choppy and the boat was lurching from side to side. Passengers on-board started looking pensive when, without warning, the boat went headlong into a rock and turned on its side. Jade fell into the water, as did all the other people on-board and a crewmember sounded the distress call. Jade had swallowed a mouthful of salt water and was floundering. Her mother and father were trying to swim towards her but their life jackets were hindering them. The water was cold and everyone was screaming. They heard the sound of a siren in the distance and could just make out the shape of a lifeboat. Within minutes, the lifeboat pulled up alongside the battered boat and the lifeboat crew hauled all the passengers from the water into the lifeboat.

Everyone was traumatised. They huddled together in blankets as the lifeboat turned around to head back to the shore. Once back on the shore, they were herded into a First-Aid Hospice to get checked over. Jade suddenly burst out crying. She'd realised that she'd lost Rose! Rose was somewhere out there in the sea, terrified and alone and she knew she'd never see her again. She couldn't stop crying.

When they flew home to Hamburg, Jade went straight to her bedroom and fell onto her bed sobbing. Her mother had phoned Marie to tell her what had happened and Marie had found it difficult to speak. She felt numb. Little Rose, who had been there to welcome her home from school every day, little Rose whom she had washed with hot soapy water on the day her father brought her home, dearest Rose who had been at her side throughout her terrible time in school was now gone. She came off the phone and sitting at the bottom of the stairs, she put her hands over her face and wept. She felt as though she was having a heart attack.

# STEFAN
## The doll maker's son

Stefan Meyer had spent a happy childhood in Rothenburg but had decided not to continue in the family business as a doll maker like his father and grandfather. Doll making required a certain skill and a sense of vocation and he simply didn't have either of those attributes towards doll making. Stefan had loved music and when he was ten his parents had bought him a piano. He excelled at it and over time became a skilled musician, giving piano lessons to local children. After finishing his degree in Music and French at University, he studied to become a primary school teacher. He had been successful in gaining a teaching post in a school in Hamburg but had decided to take a gap year before taking up the position. He was going to backpack around Europe!

Stefan had grown into a very handsome man. He had thick blonde hair, a chiselled face and bright blue eyes. Everyone warmed to Stefan. He was honest, truthful, friendly and generous. He had attained top grades at school, particularly in English, French and Music. He loved languages and was yearning to put them into practice.

The day came for him to kiss his mother and father goodbye. Luisa tried to hold back her tears but Hans couldn't control himself. He broke down as the taxi pulled up to take Stefan to the airport. Hans hugged his son to him tightly one last time as the driver placed the large rucksack in the boot. As the taxi drove off, Hans and Luisa continued waving and blowing kisses until the taxi disappeared out of sight. Hans put his arm around Luisa's shoulder and they walked slowly back into their house.

Neither of them spoke.

# Rose

## The Doll

Rose felt terrified as the waves crashed around her. She felt her head hitting a piece of rock as the current dragged her further and further out to sea. After what seemed an eternity, she felt herself getting sucked down deeper and deeper into the ocean. She was surrounded by horrible fishes who were nibbling at her dress and her hair. Her little heart was pounding as she found herself sinking faster into the deep waters. It was freezing. She knew this had to be the end. She'd never see Jade again. Something bit her leg and she felt a sudden pain and then her arm knocked against something sharp. She was in terrible agony and then she felt nothing but darkness all around her.

# Marie

Marie loved her position in the primary school. The young children she taught were very responsive to her and she always made the lessons as colourful and interesting as she could. Marie was now 30 and had still retained her sweet expression and rather sad eyes. She was pretty, slim and had a lovely attitude towards life. She loved travelling, music, reading and ballet. Her best friend was still Theresa, who had stood by her side ever since her school days. She adored Theresa. Theresa was now a mother of two little boys, one of whom was in Marie's class. Her other close friend Monika was also a lovely woman.

Marie had no desire to get married yet. She was enjoying all the challenges of her teaching post and relished every morning when she greeted all her little pupils. Marie was very observant when it came to bullying. She would remain very vigilant when on duty in the schoolyard, ensuring that no child was being victimised. She kept a careful eye out for the smallest signs of bullying and if necessary, would take the perpetrator and the victim aside to settle the issue early on.

Marie rented a small apartment in Hamburg, not far from her niece Jade. She had bought herself a little car which enabled her to get to and from the school easily. Her parents still lived in their small flat in Altona but her father had retired as a rubbish collector owing to back problems.

# Charlotte

Charlotte took up her post at the mission hospital. She had never imagined that she would see such appalling sights of children suffering from malnutrition. It was worse than anything she had seen on television or read in newspapers. The mission hospital was packed with little beds and every day she worked tirelessly with a team of fellow doctors. The diseases that were surrounding her on a daily basis worried her, in particular the frequent outbreaks of cholera and smallpox. She just hoped her immune system would stay strong enough to protect her from all of them.

Charlotte remained at the mission hospital for a further 10 years. She had never returned to Germany but had kept in touch with friends and family via email. Sophia emailed her at least twice a week with little bits of news, always suggesting that Charlotte return to Germany and take up a post working in the hospital where she worked. Charlotte was fiercely dedicated to helping these poor children at the hospice and often thought back to her own privileged upbringing. She saw how little these children had in the way of clothes, toys and access to proper food. She smiled as she recalled her childhood memories. She thought of her beautiful bedroom with the pink velvet curtains, her vast array of toys, her top-quality clothes, the hours she had spent sitting on her bed with Sophia, chatting and laughing and of course Rose. She wondered about Rose. She should never have let her mother take her to the charity shop. It was wrong and how she had regretted that decision. She wondered where Rose was now.

One day when Charlotte was tending to a little boy, she suddenly felt feverish. The doctor in charge told her to go back to her room and lie down. She returned to her room and lay down on the bed. Her whole body felt as though it was burning up. Her vision became suddenly blurred and she started seeing strange shapes dancing in front of her. Her body started to convulse and she was dripping in sweat. She was finding it hard to breathe. The shapes dancing in front of her became larger with vivid colours. She was hallucinating.

When the doctor came to check on her an hour later, Charlotte was dead.

# ROSE

## The Doll

Rose had lain at the bottom of the sea for over 10 years when suddenly it felt as though she was being strangled. She was in some sort of net and was being pulled along sitting amongst big oily fish. It was terrible. Suddenly this huge net came to the surface and for the first time in so many years, she felt sunshine on what was left of her face. Oh, it was wonderful.

The fishermen hauled the huge net onto the trawler and emptied the day's catch onto the deck. They'd done well. It was a mighty catch and they'd be able to make a fortune selling it to the market stall owners, hotels and restaurants in Marrakech. The fishes were thrown into huge ice containers, which were placed on top of each other in a refrigerated van and driven to Marrakech. The fishermen hadn't noticed the bedraggled little doll amongst all the fish!

# Stefan
## Son of the doll Maker

Stefan was enjoying his time away from the sleepy little town of Rothenburg. He would never have told his parents, but during his last few years living at home, he had found the house and the village simply suffocating. He laughed at his father, having brought his "twin brother" up from the cellar on the day he left. He had adored that little chap when he was small and had played with him for hours on end. He had kept Karl in his bedroom and they had had many imaginary conversations over the years during his early childhood. Stefan secretly admired his father's skill and craftsmanship in creating such wonderful dolls. It was a wonderful gift.

All his old toys had been put down in the cellar in the event of Stefan getting married and having children of his own. Now, after all these years, he had to remind himself of the doll's name. What on earth was it? Oh yes, he remembered it now. It was Karl.

Stefan's gap year was proving to be an amazing experience. It had surpassed all his expectations. He was having a great time. He'd met lots of interesting people and stayed in the most hilarious hostels! He'd loved Paris, Vienna, Barcelona, Venice, Lisbon – and lots more. He'd arrived in Marrakech the previous night and after a hearty breakfast he'd ambled slowly along the streets soaking up the sights and smells. After a time he decided to go and get his fortune told by a gypsy in the big main square, Jemaa el-Fnaa. He'd never had his fortune told before and thought it would be a bit of fun.

# The Fortune teller in Marrakech

The gypsy looked at Stefan's palm and said that he would fall in love with someone with whom he would be working next year. She then told him that there was something important here in Marrakech which linked him to the girl he would marry but also to his father. Stefan just smiled to be polite. The gypsy told him not to ignore her words and that she possessed a strong gift passed onto her from her grandmother of being very accurate with her intuition and readings. She told him that this link to his father and his future wife would become obvious to him very soon and that he must keep alert otherwise the chance would be lost. She said that if this object were found, it would bring enormous pleasure both to his future wife and also to his father. He paid the gypsy €10 and thought to himself that he could have spent the money on something better. He walked out of the square feeling foolish. The whole experience had been an utter load of rubbish!

## Marie

Marie felt the time had come to settle down. She had dated a lot of nice men but that special person was still to be found. She watched her schoolchildren growing up and leaving her to go on to junior school. She smiled when she thought of junior school and her lovely friendship with Theresa. That was a life-changing moment for her, one that was etched into her memory. She drove home that afternoon and sat out on her balcony and poured herself a large glass of wine. How nice it would be to meet the *right* man and start making wonderful memories together, start a family, be really happy and content. Mmm, maybe one day.

## Stefan

As Stefan strolled along the streets of Marrakech, he saw a delivery van pull up just in front of him. It nearly knocked him over! Two men quickly got out and opened the back doors. The stench was terrible! They were delivering fish to a restaurant through the kitchen entrance. He walked over to the other side of the road where there was a small pavement cafe. He sat outside and ordered a coffee and watched the two men continue to offload the cold storage boxes containing the fish.

After some time, the men came out of the kitchen entrance looking very pleased with themselves when suddenly one of the cooks rushed out of the door onto the pavement laughing his head off. He shouted to the two men whilst holding something in his hand and then threw it at them. One of the men caught it and they all started laughing. It was obviously something that had got mixed in with the fish by mistake. As the two men got back into the van, one of them threw the object out of the passenger window and it landed on the pavement. The van then drove carefully out of the alley, reversing over the object and drove off. Stefan had heard a distinct crack as the tyres went over whatever it was that had been hurled onto the floor. He continued to sip his coffee remembering the words of the fortune-teller.

# Hans and Luisa
# Stefan's Parents

Hans and Luisa carried on their lives without the company of their wonderful son. They adored Stefan. He had been a lovely little boy who seemed to just love life. He was kind and loving and they knew they'd been so lucky. Luisa knew that one day he would make a wonderful husband and father and just hoped and prayed that Stefan would meet someone as nice as himself. He deserved the best. She and Stefan had shared the most beautiful relationship. She was there when he came home from school, always willing to help him with his homework, made his favourite cakes and always encouraged him to bring friends home from school. He was sociable and funny and people were drawn to him for his lovely personality. She missed him terribly. Hans still continued to spend endless hours in the workshop making his beautiful dolls, but Luisa often felt lonely. When Stefan was home she never had that feeling of solitude but now it was acute. He had been gone for almost ten months now, but she was so pleased that he'd been enjoying himself. He had sent his parents postcards from every city he had visited and told them hilarious stories of what had happened to him on his travels. Luisa knew that he had just arrived in Marrakech.

# Marie

The head teacher announced to the staff one morning that a new teacher was starting in January. His name was Stefan Meyer from Rothenburg. The head teacher explained that Stefan was just concluding a gap year and would be returning before Christmas, ready to take up his appointment with them in January. There was a photograph of each member of staff lining the main corridor and Stefan's photograph with his name printed underneath was already up. Marie walked down the corridor during the mid-morning break and scanned the pictures. She stopped still as she studied Stefan's photograph. She'd never seen a face quite like it in all her life. It was truly beautiful.

# Stefan

Stefan finished his coffee, paid the waiter and got up. He didn't want to go over the road to examine the object but felt strangely compelled to do so. He crossed the road and to his astonishment saw what looked to be the remains of a doll. He had a pair of plastic gloves in his pocket and put those on before handling her. Judging by the fact that she had been caught by the fishermen, it was obvious that she had been in salt water for a considerable length of time. Her clothes were ravaged. Her hair and eyelashes had disappeared, one arm was fractured and her left leg was missing. Surprisingly, her right leg was intact but other than that she was a complete mess. He suddenly caught sight of the sole on her right foot where there was some kind of faint lettering.

Stefan stood in the shade of a palm tree to get out of the fierce midday sun and could just about decipher the name and address of something. He sought out another bit of shade and looking closer, realised it was his father's name and address in Rothenburg! This was unbelievable. He looked again closely at the sole of her foot but it was clearly there, albeit in very faint lettering:

*Hans Meyer, Marktplatz 91541. Rothenburg ob der Tauber, Deutschland.*

Stefan saw some faint lettering on the nape of her neck. It looked like an R but he couldn't be sure. There was an *s* and then what looked like an *e*. Could it spell Rose? It must be Rose. Stefan knew for certain that this doll would have been beautiful once and guessed that she had been made a long time before he was born, probably even before his father had met his mother. Stefan's father was a perfectionist so he knew that her hair, her clothes, her face, everything about this doll would have been meticulously crafted. Stefan could well imagine his father's reaction to what he held in his hands today. He would weep. Stefan unzipped his rucksack and carefully placed what was left of Rose in amongst his clothes. He needed to think.

He remembered his father saying that there was a wonderful doll's hospital in Berlin and that they had skilled craftsmen who could restore dolls to their original condition irrespective of how badly damaged they were. He would stay in Marrakech a few more days to visit the souks, a saffron plantation, take a camel ride through the Atlas Mountains and then fly to Berlin before returning home. He would bring his little patient to the doll's clinic to get well again.

# Puppenklinik Neukölln, Richardstrasse 99, 12044 Berlin

Stefan handed Rose over to one of the doll repairers. Herr Schneider had a kindly face and looked quite elderly. He looked down at the remains of Rose lying on the counter and then looked up at Stefan. He had never seen a doll in such a terrible state. He told Stefan that she must have lain in water for several years given her terrible condition. The fact that her head had been made from porcelain had saved her upper body but the rest of her was truly ruined. There were no facial features to be seen. Stefan was holding his breath. The Doll repairer just kept his hands spread across the counter staring at the distorted torso of what once had been a doll and shaking his head. Stefan took a deep breath and said quickly, "I can't begin to tell you what this would mean to me, if you could repair this doll. My father made it in his workshop about 30 years ago." His voice buckled when he said the words "my father".

The Doll repairer removed his glasses and looked into Stefan's eyes. "I'll do what I can for you lad but I can't promise to work a miracle. She's very badly damaged."

# Hans, Luisa and Stefan

The taxi pulled up outside his parents' house. Luisa ran out of the front door and hugged Stefan so tightly to her. Oh, how she'd missed her son. Hans stood at the doorway beaming with joy. As Stefan lugged his huge rucksack out of the boot, he looked over to his father and thought how much older he had become since he had left. Hans wrapped his arms around Stefan and buried his face into his shoulder. "Welcome home son," he whispered.

Luisa busied herself in the kitchen preparing an absolute feast for them all that evening, whilst Stefan unpacked his rucksack. After he'd given Luisa all his dirty washing he ran a lovely bath for himself and just immersed himself in it. He hadn't had a proper bath for months and as he basked in the hot soapy suds, he reflected on all the wonderful places he'd seen and all the people he'd met on his travels.

Luisa had made a wonderful meal as a homecoming and had laid the table beautifully. She had put her grandmother's embroidered tablecloth on the table with a vase of huge stargazer lilies. A big pot of *Sauerbraten* (beef stew) stood to one side of the flowers and a plate of *Kartoffelpuffer (*potato pancakes) on the other side. A large basket of freshly baked brötchen was on the table with fresh creamy butter. Luisa poured them all a glass of excellent white wine. Hans raised his glass and said "Prosit" and then they tucked into their wonderful supper.

It was a wonderful evening. Stefan talked about all the places he'd visited and some of the hovels he'd ended up staying in! Hans and Luisa had never laughed so much in ages. Stefan was a brilliant narrator of stories and Luisa thought how lucky the children in the primary school were going to be to have her son as their teacher. They'd love him, just as she did.

After supper, they sat around the fire and Stefan took the opportunity of asking his father about Rose. He didn't want to mention her name so he carefully raised the subject of dolls in general. He asked his father whether he had ever created a doll that he had almost felt was human. Hans looked startled. "How strange of you to ask me that, Stefan. Yes, I did. Her name was Rose. I made her, oh, let me think; it must have been over thirty years ago. Oh, she was the sweetest thing – *ein kleiner Schatz.* I remember her vividly."

Stefan looked at his father and said, "Papi, can you remember what she looked like?"

"Of course I remember!" Hans told Stefan how he had given her thick auburn hair with two plaits which he let hang loosely over each shoulder. He had given her a very sweet, almost angelic expression, orange coloured lips, long brown eyelashes and ribbons in her hair. He couldn't quite recall the dress she wore but knew it was greenish in colour. His face suddenly clouded over and Luisa asked him what was wrong. He told them how he recalled the day he had left Rose in the front window of Frau Winkelmann's shop and felt so worried for her. Stefan asked him why. Hans said that he had had a premonition that life would turn out tough for her. He looked embarrassed when he told Stefan and Luisa that he had sewn a little red velvet heart inside her. He blushed and his eyes filled with tears. In that moment Stefan wanted to kiss him.

The following morning, Stefan telephoned Herr Schneider to tell him what Rose had once looked like. He described in great detail everything his father had told him the previous evening. Herr Schneider listened without uttering a word, writing down carefully what Stefan was telling him. "Is that everything Stefan?" Stefan took a deep breath. "My father sewed a little red velvet heart inside her Herr Schneider". Stefan shut his eyes and bit his lip. There was a long silence on the other end.

"That shouldn't be a problem Stefan" said Herr Schneider quietly.

# Stefan and Marie at the
# Primary School

Stefan had rented an apartment just outside the centre of Hamburg in Wedel. He had arrived in Hamburg a week before starting his new appointment at the primary school. Luisa and Hans had helped him settle in and Luisa had made sure he had plenty of food in the cupboards and that the fridge was full. He felt good here. The last time he had lived alone was in student accommodation, but this felt much nicer.

His first day at the school had been overwhelming. The headmaster had introduced him to all the staff and he felt very welcome. After his first week of teaching he felt more at ease with everything because one of the teachers had taken the time to explain the workings and principles of the school to him. Her name was Marie.

Stefan spent the following weekend marking 37 essays sitting on his comfy sofa in his new flat. He was happy enough although deep down he wanted someone special in his life. He got up to put the kettle on when suddenly his phone rang. It was Herr Schneider. The doll was ready to be collected.

Stefan arranged a day the following week when he had a free afternoon and took the train to Berlin. He went straight to the Puppenklinik where he was greeted warmly by Herr Schneider. He was led into a room and told to wait. After five minutes, Herr Schneider appeared in the room with a large package, closed the door behind him, sat down opposite Stefan and proceeded to open it.

# Marie

Marie sat in her apartment after a hard day in school. Her mind wandered to Stefan and hoped he was having a nice time in Berlin. She had been in the staff room when he announced he was going to Berlin but he hadn't given the reason. She really liked Stefan. There was something very special about this man, something deep. He had a soul. She thought of her little Rose. She had had a face with such soul, such depth. She had lost touch with her niece, Jade after the family decided to move to France. Jade's father had been offered an excellent job with a fantastic salary so they hadn't hesitated. They loved living in France. Marie remembered that day so clearly when Jade's mother had phoned her to tell her that Rose had fallen overboard in the waters of Essaouira. She had managed to remain calm on the phone for Jade's sake but when she put the phone down she had sobbed and sobbed. It was the worst news she'd ever had.

## Herr Schneider at the Dolls Hospital in Berlin

Herr Schneider carefully unwrapped the brown paper and lifted out the most beautiful doll Stefan had ever seen. Stefan remembered watching his father create hundreds of dolls but he'd never seen anything as wonderful as this. He was speechless. He couldn't believe that the remains of Rose could ever have been restored to such magnificent beauty. He looked up at Herr Schneider and the words wouldn't come out. This elderly man with the kindest face had made a miracle happen. Herr Schneider handed Rose over to Stefan and Stefan held her as though he had the most precious thing in all the world. Now he understood completely his father's love for this little doll. He understood how he must have felt leaving her in that shop in Munich. He understood it all. As he left the shop, Herr Schneider thanked him for his payment and said, "Don't forget that your little Rose has had her heart repaired too. I managed to find some red velvet!" Stefan smiled. "Danke Herr Schneider. I'll never forget what you've done." They shook hands. Stefan boarded the train back to Hamburg, never having felt so happy in all his life. This was a day he would never forget.

## Marie and Stefan

After a few weeks, the attraction between Marie and Stefan was obvious. All the staff in the school could see that they were destined for one another and it was lovely to see. They had started dating about two weeks after Stefan had taken up his post at the school. Sometimes Stefan would go over to Marie's flat or sometimes she would pop over to Wedel to see him. They loved being in each other's company and with their arms wrapped around one another, they would talk into the early hours about so many things. They were soulmates in every sense of the word. Sometimes if they were at Marie's flat, Marie would light little candles and they'd sit on her balcony with a big blanket wrapped around them, sipping a glass of good wine. They would look up and watch the stars come out and talk non-stop. They were so in love. One evening, they were talking about their childhoods and Marie told Stefan that her school days had been painful until Theresa came into her life. Her one solace had been a doll that she once had. Her mouth started to quiver. "Tell me about her," Stefan said. Marie started from the beginning from her father finding her in a black bag outside a charity shop about twenty years ago, to living with Marie, then passing her on to Jade and then to that fateful day on the boat. She put her hands over her face. "You wouldn't believe how I miss that little doll Stefan, even now, after all these years. She was my rock." Stefan squeezed her hand. "What was the name of your doll Marie?" he asked gently. "Rose. Her name was Rose" she whispered.

## Rose

Rose thought she'd come back from the dead! This was a resurrection in its truest form. She could feel again! She felt marvellous! She remembered nothing of that fateful day, only the water. She knew she had died when she landed at the bottom of the ocean as she had felt her heart being eaten by a large fish but she had been given another chance. She wanted to dance with joy. Maybe she'd even see Marie again! Once she had felt Herr Schneider put the last stitch of the heart inside her she felt alive again. She had been given another chance!

# The Wedding

The day arrived for Stefan and Marie to get married. They were having a church ceremony in Hamburg and all the staff from the school came as well as their parents and friends. Hans and Louisa looked very elegant. Louisa had treated herself to a huge pink hat with peacock feathers and felt amazing. Stefan looked at his mother and thought she had never looked so beautiful. Helmut and Elizabeth also looked lovely although Helmut now needed a stick to walk with. Theresa was in the congregation with her husband and children and even Jacob, the violin maker from Rothenburg, had come along with his daughter Klara and her little boy. It was a beautiful day in every way. The sun was shining, the church bells were ringing, the organ sounded majestic and the couple looked radiant as they came out of the church. Everyone threw garlands of flowers and confetti at them and the moment was theirs. Marie looked like an angel. Her wedding dress was beautiful but she had chosen a wreath of wildflowers for her headdress instead of a veil. Stefan simply looked like a film star. They made a beautiful couple.

At the wedding reception, the bride and groom took their places at the top table. Before the speeches began, Stefan stood up and announced that he had a little gift for his wife. Marie looked puzzled. Stefan handed her a beautifully wrapped present with a big red bow and asked her to open it. Stefan then sat down. There was silence in the hall as the guests watched Marie untie the big red bow and then open the wrapping paper. She gasped! The guests waited with baited breath as Marie held Rose in her hands. She started to cry but they were tears of absolute joy. Stefan put his hand on her shoulder. Hans looked over and thought he was seeing things. Stefan stood up and addressed the wedding guests.

"Ladies and Gentlemen, I want to tell you a story today of a little miracle which began in my father's workshop over 30 years ago."

Marie was holding Rose in just the same way she had done when she had been a child. She didn't hear Stefan's words as they echoed through the hall, she only saw Rose. Oh, how she had missed that sad beautiful face. She was back to being an eight-year-old girl again, scared and timid in the schoolyard but then she looked up at her husband and felt such enormous gratitude to have him in her life and at the miracle of having Rose again. Marie looked across the room to find Jade, who had flown over from France to attend the wedding of her favourite Auntie. Jade had her hand over her mouth in absolute shock and Marie smiled at her through her tears. At the end of the speech, Stefan raised a toast to Herr Schneider from the Puppenklinik Neukölln in Berlin. Everybody stood up. Marie now looked radiant and blew him a kiss from across the room. Herr Schneider smiled and raised his glass.

# Hans
# (The Doll Maker)

Hans had never quite recovered from Stefan's speech at the wedding. He and Luisa adored Marie and watching her reaction to Rose had brought him to his knees. What a story! How fate had brought Stefan to Marrakech and then that fortune teller? He knew, yes he knew, that Rose was going to have a hard journey through life. He had felt it at the moment he had seen the little girl take the carrier bag from Frau Winkelmann all those years ago. My word, how many years ago was it? Hans guessed it to be over thirty years ago. He wished he knew what had happened, for Rose to have ended up in a charity shop, as the little girl in Frau Winkelmann's shop had looked so sweet. He thought her name was Charlotte but couldn't be sure. He remembered her father. Strangely enough, Hans had packed Stefan's old doll Karl for Stefan to pass on to his children if they had a little boy. He had left it in Stefan's flat in a box before he and Luisa returned to Rothenburg after the wedding.

# Twins

Stefan and Marie moved out of their respective flats into a bigger rented house. They continued to work at the primary school and life was good. Marie became pregnant a few months later and gave birth to a set of beautiful twins. Stefan and Marie were thrilled to bits! They decorated the nursery in pale blue and lemon, as they knew they were having a boy and a girl.

The two dolls took pride of place on the large windowsill, basking in the warm sunlight. Underneath the windowsill were two large wicker cribs each with a porcelain plaque bearing their names. Written on the pink plaque was the name Rose and written on the blue plaque was the name Karl. They couldn't have been named anything else!

*"There are two ways to live:*
*You can live as though nothing is a miracle or you can live as though*
*everything is a miracle."*

Albert Einstein.